Rabbit Gets Lost

Disney's
Winnie the Pooh First Readers

Pooh Gets Stuck
Bounce, Tigger, Bounce!
Pooh's Pumpkin
Rabbit Gets Lost
Pooh's Honey Tree
Happy Birthday, Eeyore!
Pooh's Best Friend

Disney's

A Winnie the Pooh First Reader

Rabbit Gets Lost

Adapted by Isabel Gaines

ILLUSTRATED BY Studio Orlando

DISNEY
PRESS

NEW YORK

Based on the Pooh Stories by A. A. Milne (copyright The Pooh Properties Trust).

First Edition

1 3 5 7 9 10 8 6 4 2

Library of Congress Cataloging-in-Publication Data
Gaines, Isabel.
Rabbit gets lost / adapted by Isabel Gaines.
p.   cm. — (Winnie the Pooh first reader)
Summary: Thinking that Tigger is just too bouncy, Rabbit, Piglet, and Pooh
take him out to the forest to give him a scare.
ISBN: 0-7868-4254-7
[1. Toys—Fiction. 2. Lost children—Fiction.] I. Title. II. Series.
PZ7.M3365ab   1998
[E]—dc21   97-48914

For more Disney Press fun, visit www.DisneyBooks.com

Rabbit Gets Lost

Rabbit was in his garden,

picking carrots.

Suddenly . . .

BOING!

Rabbit landed flat on his back.

The carrots flew out
of his hands.

Rabbit looked up at Tigger
and sighed.

"Oh, Tigger," said Rabbit,

"won't you ever stop bouncing?"

"Nope!" said Tigger.

"Bouncing is what Tiggers

do best."

That afternoon, Rabbit had

a chat with Piglet and Pooh.

"We need to unbounce

Tigger," Rabbit said.

"But how?" Pooh asked.

"We'll take him

for a long walk

in the woods," Rabbit said.

"Then we'll lose him!"

Pooh frowned.

"Losing someone doesn't seem

like a very friendly thing to do."

"Don't worry," Rabbit said.

"We'll find him again—

after a while."

"But by then," Rabbit said,
"he'll be a less bouncy Tigger.
A small and sad Tigger.
An oh-Rabbit-am-I-glad-
to-see-you Tigger."

Rabbit smiled at the thought.

Early the next morning,

Pooh, Piglet, Rabbit,

and Tigger set off

on their walk.

It was cold and damp

in the Hundred-Acre Wood.

The mist was so thick

no one could see a thing.

No one but Tigger, that is.

He kept bouncing

over the mist.

Tigger bounced circles
around his friends.
Finally, he bounced off
into the woods.

"Quick!" Rabbit cried.

"Everybody hide!

Now is our chance to lose

Tigger!"

Rabbit hid in a hollow log.

Piglet and Pooh squeezed in

beside him.

Tigger bounced into view.

"Hey, you guys!" he yelled.

"Where are you?"

Tigger bounced off again.

Rabbit popped out of the log.

"Hooray!" he cheered.

"He's gone. Quick!

Let's all go home."

"It's funny how everything
looks the same in the mist,"
Rabbit said awhile later.
"I think we passed
that sandpit a few
minutes ago."

"We did," Pooh agreed.

"Well, it's lucky I know the

forest so well," Rabbit said.

"Otherwise, we might get lost."

Piglet shivered in the mist.

As far as he could tell,

they were lost!

"Don't worry," Rabbit said.

"Just follow me."

And so they did.

Again . . .

and again . . .

and again.

Right back to the same old

sandpit.

"I have an idea," Pooh said.

"Every time we look for home,

we find this sandpit.

Maybe if we try looking

for the sandpit,

we'll find home instead!"

"Don't be silly," Rabbit said.
"If I walk away from this pit
and then walk back,
of course I'll find it."
And to prove his point,
he walked away.

Pooh and Piglet waited at the
sandpit for Rabbit to return.
They waited, and waited,
and waited.
Pooh's tummy began to rumble.

"I'm hungry," Pooh said.

"I think we should go home

and have some lunch."

"But we don't know the way,"

Piglet pointed out.

"Do we?"

"Well, I left twelve pots
of honey in my cupboard,"
Pooh said.

"And each one
is calling me home.
All we have to do
is follow my tummy."
And so they did.

On their way home,

Piglet and Pooh bumped

into Tigger.

"Where have you been?"

Tigger asked.

"And where's old long ears?"

"I'm afraid we've lost him,"

Pooh said sadly.

"Don't worry," Tigger said.

"I'll find him."

And off he bounced again.

Just in time.

For at that very minute,

poor Rabbit was in great need

of finding.

The mist was getting mistier.

The woods were getting woodsier.

And Rabbit was getting scared!

RIBBIT!

A big frog croaked.

Rabbit's heart began to pound.

WOOOOO!

A cold wind howled.

Rabbit's heart beat faster.

But when he heard the loudest

noise of all, Rabbit stopped

being scared.

BOING!

Rabbit knew what that meant.

He ran toward Tigger.

"Tigger!" Rabbit cried.

"You're supposed to be lost!"

Tigger bounced toward Rabbit.

"Oh, Tiggers never get lost,"

he said.

Then he offered his tail

to Rabbit.

Rabbit grabbed Tigger's tail.

He held on tight

as Tigger led him through

the mist and mud.

Rabbit was now a small and sad
Rabbit.

A lost and found Rabbit.

But most of all,

he was an oh-Tigger-
am-I-glad-to-see-you Rabbit!